Illustrations created by mouth painting artist Ian Parker,
working in collaboration with author Victor Margiotta.

*This book is dedicated to Mary, Holly and Emily, who have
shown me such love and support, and to the rest of my family.*
Illustrator – Ian Parker

My special thanks to Carmen, who never stopped believing.
Author – Victor Margiotta

Dreams can come true,
although sometimes in the
most unexpected ways.

It was late afternoon on a hot summer's day and a young boy could be seen racing through a field of golden corn.

Danny loved to run and he was heading towards the tall, dark trees of the forest that he could see in the distance. As he ran, beautiful butterflies fluttered and birds swooped around his head, screeching his name in welcome. "Danny, Danny," they cried.

Danny raced out of the bright sunshine and entered into the coolness of the forest to follow the winding pathway that would lead him to his special tree.

Many familiar friends were there to greet him. A long-eared rabbit stopped nibbling on grass shoots and a mole interrupted its digging, raising their heads to acknowledge his arrival. "Hello Mr. Rabbit. Hello Mr. Mole," said Danny.

"How are you all?" he said affectionately to the deer, the raccoon and the squirrels, who were scampering up and down the tree trunk. "What a racket you are making today Mr. Woodpecker," said Danny, as he watched the bird's sharp beak hammering into the tree.

Using his strong arms and legs Danny began to climb up towards the viewing platform built high up in the tree.

And suddenly, there before him, was what made the tree so special; a view he thought was the most beautiful on earth.

More friends started to arrive. Red squirrels with long, bushy tails scurried along the branches towards him; parrots feeding on the bright red berries squawked their hellos. "Good day squirrels. How are you today my noisy parrot friends?"

Even the wide-eyed tawny owl peered out of his nest in the adjoining tree to see what all the commotion was about. "Sorry if I woke you too early Mr. Owl," said Danny. It was a bit too soon in the day for the owl to pay too much attention though and he quickly slipped back into his warm, cosy home to continue with his much-needed sleep.

Danny then laid down to rest and quickly drifted off to sleep. Soon he was lost in his regular dream of becoming an Olympic champion. As usual his dream ended with him standing on the winner's podium, with a gold medal dangling around his neck. While all around the stadium, a huge crowd chanted his name, "Danny, Danny."

Danny woke up with a jolt as one of the squirrels on the branch above dropped a nut that landed with a BOING close to his head. His dream broken, Danny then began to have sad thoughts about the recent loss of his devoted mother and how his carefree, loving life with her around had been replaced by harder times, living with his strict and heartless uncle. Which suddenly reminded him that he was late and needed to get back fast, so as not to anger his uncle.

BOING

Running as quickly as his legs would carry him and gasping for breath, Danny arrived back at the house where he could see his uncle standing impatiently next to a huge tree trunk lying on the ground, ready for him to chop. He shouted in Danny's direction, "You're late, get to work."

Danny immediately began chopping the logs that his uncle sold at the local market. It was back-breaking work but Danny never complained.

CHOP

CHOP CHOP

CHOP

For Danny, going to school was a welcome relief from chopping logs every day and he'd always run there and back as fast as he could, rather than take the bus.

Once a week the children would participate in sports and Danny's preference was always for the running classes. He was by far the fastest runner at his school and the other boys could often be heard pleading with the teacher, "Please Sir, give us a chance... Danny's too quick for us."

But, after school, it was straight back home to chop more logs for Danny and if he did have a moment to spare, he'd always head for his special tree in the forest.

"Danny"

"Danny"

T hen one day, Danny finished his work earlier than normal, seizing the opportunity to go off to the forest while his uncle was in town for the afternoon.

Arriving at his special tree, his friends were all there to greet him as usual and he quickly climbed up to the wooden platform. "Danny, Danny," cried the parrots and parakeets. "Good afternoon my noisy friends," he replied warmly, as he laid down to rest.

Danny soon drifted off to sleep and once again he began dreaming about being an Olympic Champion. He could hear the race commentator's voice in his dream... "And as they race into the finishing straight, Danny is coming up fast on the outside and as they lunge for the line it's…"

THUD

Many hours later Danny was found lying at the base of his special tree. Had it not been for the commotion created by the parrots screeching his name "Danny, Danny," who were alarmed at seeing their friend lying motionless on the ground, the local woodsman would not have found him. Looking down at the boy it was immediately obvious that he needed to get him to the hospital, and fast.

Danny spent many weeks recovering in hospital but after a while he started to grow concerned. He couldn't feel his legs even when he pinched them and he hadn't walked once since arriving at the hospital.

Then, one afternoon, his doctor broke the bad news he had been dreading since the accident. His back, that was so severely damaged in the fall, meant he would never be able to use his legs again. Shocked, the words gradually sank in. If I cannot use my legs I cannot walk again and that means I cannot run again, thought Danny, as tears began to roll down his cheeks.

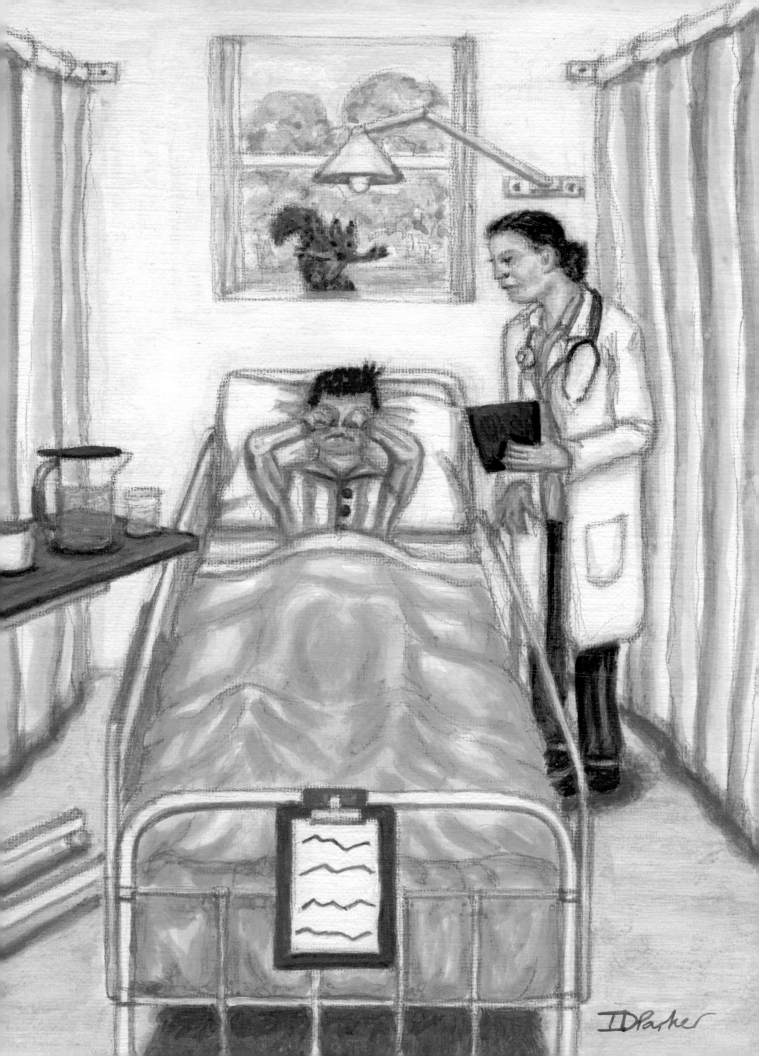

Now confined to a wheelchair, Danny left the hospital to go back to live with his uncle. But soon it became clear that since he could no longer chop logs from a wheelchair, he was of little use to his uncle. Then one day his uncle took him to one side and said, "Listen, I've decided you'd be better off if you went to live with your Grandma. She can look after you better than me."

So that was it, decision taken and Danny's new life would now be spent with his Grandma, who lived in a house nearby.

When he arrived at her cottage, Danny was warmly greeted by his Grandma, who gave him a hug and a kiss on the cheek. This attention annoyed her little dog Billy, who began to bark at this newcomer in the wheelchair.

"Come in Danny, welcome to your new home," said Grandma, affectionately.

Once settled in his new bedroom, Danny could hear his Grandma singing and he could smell the delicious aroma of the freshly baked bread and cakes she was preparing in the kitchen.

As Danny entered the kitchen he could not believe his eyes as he looked at the wonderful spread of food that his Grandma had prepared to welcome him.

In time Danny settled well into his new home. He enjoyed the love and attention from Grandma, which reminded him of his mother. Billy had also become a close companion and wherever Danny went, there he was padding along beside him.

But Danny found it hard to accept his new life in a wheelchair. Not being able to run anymore, or visit his special tree and knowing that it meant he could never realise his dream of becoming an Olympic champion.

Danny spent most of his free time wheeling himself aimlessly around the garden. Then one day a small girl's face appeared over the fence. "Hello, my name's Katie, do you live next door now?" she said.

"Yes, I do, my name's Danny and this is Billy," he replied.

"If you don't mind me saying so, you seem a bit unhappy," said Katie.

"I can't walk or run anymore and it makes me feel sad," he said and immediately began wheeling himself down towards the end of the garden.

"Let's be friends Danny," she called after him, before diving back behind the fence.

Danny had never ventured to the end of the garden before and there in front of him, almost hidden from view, was an old, broken down stone building covered in creeping ivy.

Intrigued, he decided to go inside to explore and headed for the old wooden door. Turning the rusted handle, the door creaked open. As he rolled his chair through the doorway, he entered into a dusty, gloomy, cobwebby interior. It had the musty smell of a place not visited for years and Billy was sniffing the air nervously beside him.

At the far end of the building Danny could see a dark, dusty sheet that appeared to be hiding something. He moved closer to investigate and immediately Billy began to bark and growl and the hairs on his body began to stand on end. Something was bothering him but Danny was curious to see what was hidden under the sheet. As he pulled the sheet back, a shaft of light suddenly shot through a broken glass window revealing a very old and unusual looking wheelchair. The chair was gently vibrating and by now Billy was extremely agitated and barking loudly at this strange object.

Although feeling nervous, Danny was fascinated by the wheelchair and moving himself closer he used his strong arms to lift himself onto the pulsing chair. As he lowered himself on to the seat, it started to make a hissing sound and the hissing became even louder as the chair began to change beneath him.

Suddenly the dusty old chair took on a shiny, metallic appearance. The frame became sleek and powerful as it began to take on a new shape and the wheels started to transform as the hubs began to sprout metallic, gold wings. Billy was going crazy now but Danny was delighted. "Wow, what a machine!" he shouted.

Leaving his own wheelchair behind, Danny wheeled himself out into the garden in the amazing new chair. As he pumped his arms faster, the metallic wings sprouting from the wheel hubs grew slightly longer and more powerful and soon Danny was outside the house and hurtling along the road with Billy in hot pursuit. The birds were delighted to see their friend again, crying "Danny, Danny," as they swooped around him in his magic wheelchair.

"Danny"

"Danny"

When Danny eventually returned home, Grandma and Katie were both waiting anxiously at the door. They were surprised to see him in his amazing new wheelchair and he immediately started to explain how he had found it.

That night, exhausted from his incredible day, it was time to sleep. Danny parked the magic wheelchair as close as he could to his bedside, excited about the day ahead.

Waking up the next morning, having hardly slept a wink thinking about his new chair, Danny was shocked to see Billy fast asleep in the battered old wheelchair that now sat next to his bed. "What's happened to my magic wheelchair?" he shouted, waking Billy up with a start.

Danny suddenly started to feel sad and began to wonder whether the magic wheelchair had all been a dream too. Pushing Billy down, he decided to lift himself onto the old wheelchair and as soon as he sat down on the seat, it suddenly began to come alive again. You see, the magic wheelchair only responded when Danny sat in it and soon it had transformed itself into the sleek, magical wheelchair of yesterday. "My chair is back, my chair is back," he cried, hardly able to contain his excitement.

After breakfast, Danny went outside the house, where he was greeted by Katie. "Good morning Danny, that really is a beautiful wheelchair," she said. "Isn't it just; want to watch me put it through its paces?" he replied. She nodded, so off he went with Billy running along behind.

Danny's life was transformed by the magic wheelchair and every day became like a new adventure. Now back at school Danny proudly displayed his new wheelchair to his friends. They all gathered around him to admire the new machine and one of the boys let out a low whistle, saying ... "Nice wheels Danny."

Danny continued to race against the other boys at school but in this new wheelchair he was still far too quick for them. However, this extraordinary talent did not go unnoticed among Danny's school teachers, who all decided it would be

better for him if he raced against other, young wheelchair athletes from the surrounding the area.

Before long Danny was racing against young wheelchair racers from other local schools, with his biggest supporters, Grandma, Katie and Billy proudly looking on. But none of the local children were fast enough to be able to compete with Danny and before long his teachers felt it necessary to enter him in regional schools' championships; this time racing against much older boys.

Danny won all of these races very easily too and eventually it was decided he needed to be given an even greater challenge by entering him in the country's national championships, against men of all age groups. But amazingly, he came out on top again.

But in spite of all this success, there was still something missing for Danny. Every night since his accident he had continued to dream about being an Olympic champion. Just as he had done, so many times before, when he had slept up in his special tree in the forest.

Then, one day, he received a letter, that came by special delivery. The kindly postman handed him the letter saying, "Better open this, young man, looks pretty important."

He ripped open the envelope and inside was a letter confirming that he had been selected to represent his country at the next Paralympic Games. "Grandma, Grandma," he shouted, "It's really happening, it's really happening," thrusting the letter in front of her to read. "Well done Danny, I'm so proud of you," she said, giving him a big hug.

The months that followed saw Danny racing around in his magic wheelchair in preparation for the big Olympic event. The birds had no problem keeping up with him but poor Billy did and he was always grateful when Danny stopped the wheelchair and allowed him to jump up onto his lap to finish the training.

Soon the big day arrived and Danny waited nervously on the start line with the other competitors. He was the youngest ever competitor for a Paralympic final and he felt quite small next to the grown men he was racing against. With 60,000 spectators cheering the racers, the noise was deafening.

From the start of the race Danny positioned himself near the back, to ensure he did not use up his energy too soon. With two laps to go he could hear the roar of the crowd, as he started to make his move. Entering the final lap Danny was still back in fourth place and he was beginning to feel tired. He was, after all, battling against the best wheelchair racers in the world.

Danny began to have doubts about whether he could make it, when seemingly out of nowhere he could hear the distant, reassuring voice of his mother saying, *You can do it Danny. This is your dream, make it come true.*

Suddenly, his arms made so strong by the endless chopping of logs for his uncle, began to pump faster and as they did, the wings of the magic chair began to grow longer. Approaching the finishing straight the powerful, metallic wings started to sweep back like an aeroplane, lifting the chair so that it was

barely touching the ground. One by one he began to pass the other racers but half way down the finishing straight there was still one competitor in front of him and Danny was now almost flying above the track as he raced towards the finish line. With one final push he lunged the wheelchair at the finishing tape as they crossed the line, locked together. Exhausted and slumped in his chair, Danny had no idea who had won the race until he heard the huge crowd chanting his name, "Danny, Danny, Danny."

It was only later, when he was on the winner's podium receiving his gold medal, that Danny began to fully appreciate that he had, at last, achieved his dream to be an Olympic champion. A dream that had begun when he slept up in his special tree, deep in the forest.

Back outside Danny's home, people from the surrounding towns gathered to welcome their champion. Among the cheering crowd he could see the doctor, the postman and the woodsman and many of his closest friends from school. Sat in front of the crowd proudly wearing his gold medal, Danny leaned across to his uncle who was enthusiastically leading the cheering and said, "Glad you could make it Uncle. Without you pushing me so hard, I would never have been strong enough to be a Paralympic champion."

So all was forgiven and everyone Danny most wanted to share his Olympic success with were there, right by his side. Grandma, Katie, Uncle and Billy and not to forget, some of his friends from the forest. All were incredibly proud of their local hero.

THE END

The Story Behind Danny's Dream

Danny's Dream was created through a collaboration between illustrator Ian Parker, a mouth painter with the Mouth and Foot Painting Artists (MFPA) and author, Victor Margiotta.

The idea for the book was initially sparked when Victor watched the inspirational Paralympians competing at the Olympic Games. Having worked alongside the MFPA artists for many years and seeing first hand the inspiring art they produce, it occurred to him that if these two elements could be brought together, it could form the basis of a truly unique children's book.

The resulting book is based on a young boy called Danny, who dreams of becoming an Olympic champion. Following an accident his life is transformed but in spite of becoming disabled, he never gives up on his dream.

This is the first time a disabled artist has been involved in the creation of a children's book, that features a disabled boy as its central character. The artist, Ian Parker, produced the illustrations by holding a paintbrush in his mouth, giving a very distinctive feel to the book.

Critically, the book delivers a charming, magical story that is full of hope and delightful imagery that will have huge appeal for children; whilst at the same time conveying important and engaging underlying messages about diversity and inclusivity.